by Anna Kang illustrated by Christoph...

Can I Tell You a Secret?

Yes, you.
Hi.

Could you come
here for a sec?

I have a SECRET.

Can you *keep* a secret?
You sure?
Because I don't want
anyone else to know.
Do you *promise*?

Thanks.

I knew I could count on you.

My secret is...
I can't swim.
Not even a little bit.
And...
I'm afraid of the water.

You're probably thinking,
"But you're a *frog*."
I know. But I'm afraid.
I have been ever since
I was a tadpole.

How did I keep this a secret
for so long?
Good question.

A lot of quick thinking...

and hard work.

It's exhausting.

And I'm very sad.
Because I really
want to swim.
I'm a frog, after all!
What should I do?

What's that? You think
I should tell someone?
Like my parents?
Are you sure? POSITIVE?
You wouldn't lie to me, right?

OK... Maybe you're right.

How about I tell them tomorrow?

OK, OK.
I'll do it now.

Mum? Dad? I have something
to tell you. I'm... I...

...I thought dinner was just FANTASTIC!

Well, dinner really WAS tasty. What? You think I should try again? (Sigh.) OK... If you say so.

Mum? Dad? I'm... I...

Yes, Monty?

...I'm really glad you're my parents.

Thanks, buddy. You're awesome too.

We love you, Montague.

Why are you
looking at me
like that?
I really AM glad
they're my parents!
All right, all right...
I'll tell them.

Mum? Dad? I
have something
important to
tell you.
I... I'm...

I'm afraid of the water.

I'm so scared.
Are you sure I can do this?
OK.
Will you stay with me?
Thanks.

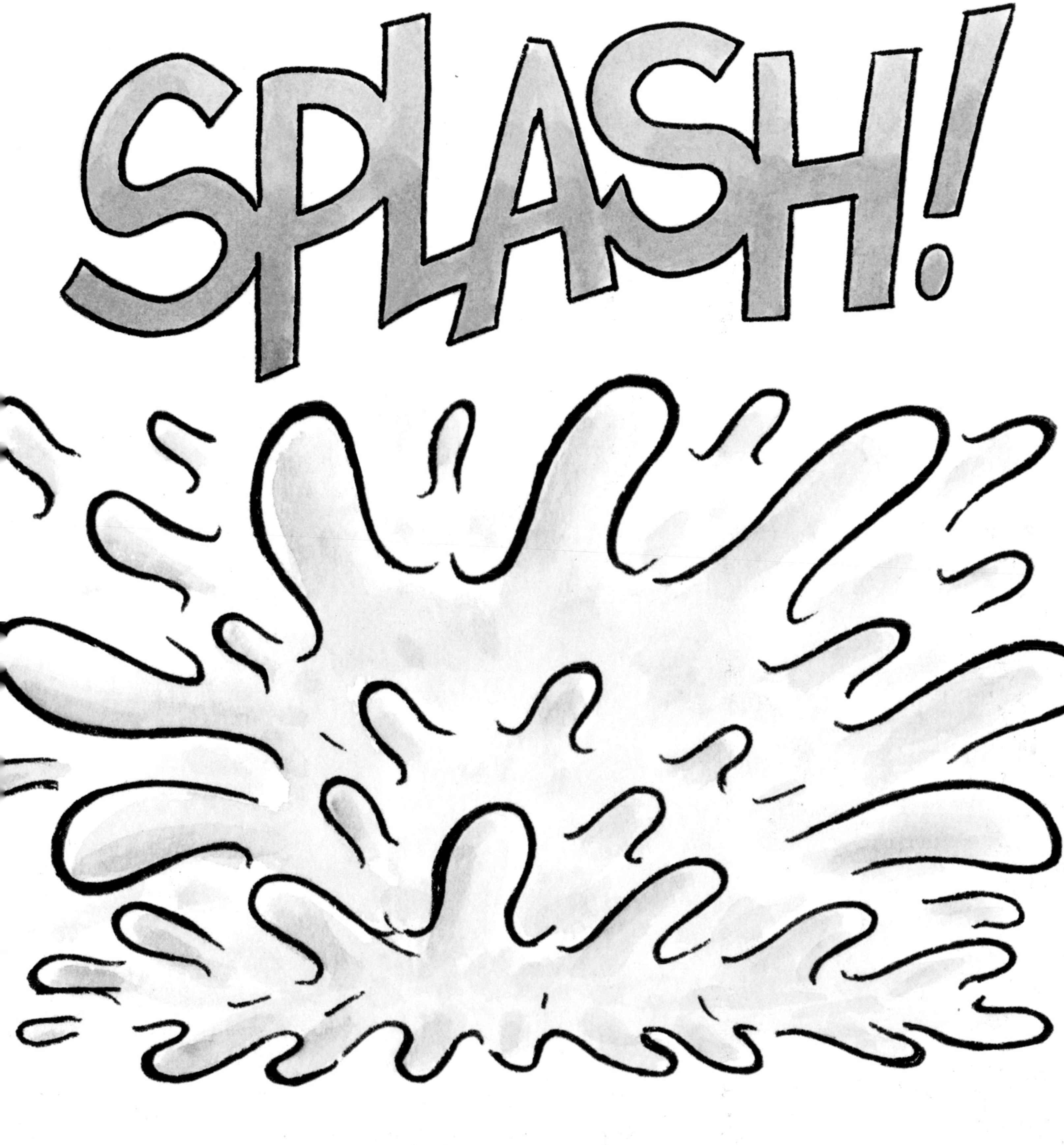
SPLASH!

I did it!
Thanks for being such
a great friend.
Can you come back
again tomorrow?

To Emil, Lisa, and Emma, with love
—**Anna & Chris**

HODDER CHILDREN'S BOOKS

This edition published in Great Britain in 2016 by Hodder and Stoughton.
Originally published by HarperCollins, Inc. Used with permission of
Pippin Properties, Inc. through Rights People, London.

A CIP catalogue record of this book
is available from the British Library.

HB ISBN: 978 1 444 92641 5
PB ISBN: 978 1 444 92643 9

10 9 8 7 6 5 4 3 2 1

Printed and bound in China.

FSC
www.fsc.org
MIX
Paper from
responsible sources
FSC® C104740

Hodder Children's Books
An imprint of
Hachette Children's Group
Part of Hodder and Stoughton
Carmelite House
50 Victoria Embankment
London EC4Y 0DZ

An Hachette UK Company
www.hachette.co.uk

www.hachettechildrens.co.uk